A dark curtain of silky hair blew over Rosa's face. Then her stomach swooshed as the snow twister swept her from her feet and twirled her high into the air. "We're off to the Glittering Cavern!" she cried.

★ ➤

# LOOK OUT FOR MORE ADVENTURES AT

## UNICORN ACADEMY

Sophia and Rainbow

Scarlett and Blaze

Ava and Star

Isabel and Cloud

Layla and Dancer

Olivia and Snowflake

Rosa and Crystal

Ariana and Whisper

★ ⋆ ★

# UNICORN ACADEMY
## Rosa and Crystal

# JULIE SYKES
### illustrated by LUCY TRUMAN

A STEPPING STONE BOOK™
Random House 🏠 New York

Text copyright © 2019 by Julie Sykes and Linda Chapman
Cover art and interior illustrations copyright © 2019 by Lucy Truman

Random House and the colophon are registered trademarks and A Stepping Stone Book and the colophon are trademarks of Penguin Random House LLC.

Visit us on the Web! rhcbooks.com

Educators and librarians, for a variety of teaching tools, visit us at
RHTeachersLibrarians.com

Library of Congress Cataloging-in-Publication Data is available upon request.
ISBN 978-0-593-17945-1 (trade) — ISBN 978-0-593-17946-8 (lib. bdg.)
ISBN 978-0-593-17947-5 (ebook)

Printed in the United States of America
10 9 8 7 6 5
First American Edition

To Fiona and Kirsty,
who make the magic happen

reason Ms. Rosemary had stopped picking her and kept asking the others instead. Rosa couldn't understand it.

"Well done," Crystal whispered, her warm breath tickling Rosa's face.

"Thanks!" Rosa stroked Crystal's sleek white neck, patterned with swirls of shimmery pink. Crystal was extremely pretty, and Rosa had been thrilled when Ms. Nettles, the head teacher, had paired

"Good work, Rosa. Crystal is the cleanest unicorn I've seen today, and those silver ribbons look very pretty in her blue-and-purple mane and tail—a very good choice!"

"Thank you, Ms. Rosemary." Rosa blushed, her heart swelling with pride. She'd been at Unicorn Academy for a month now, and she had been worrying recently that she'd done something to upset Ms. Rosemary, the Care of Unicorns teacher. Rosa loved being the best at things, and even though she always put her hand up first to answer questions or volunteer for jobs, for some

them together on their first day at the academy. Crystal was always happy to go along with whatever Rosa wanted to do, and they'd become friends immediately.

Ms. Rosemary continued to inspect the other unicorns. The class was made up of the five girls from Diamond dorm—Rosa's dorm—as well as the students from Topaz and Ruby dorms.

"Whisper's mane is braided perfectly, Ariana," Ms. Rosemary said approvingly to the girl next to Rosa. Serious Ariana, who was always neat and tidy and whose clothes were spotlessly clean, looked very pleased.

"But, Matilda . . . oh dear!" Ms. Rosemary shook her head as she inspected Pearl, Matilda's unicorn. The braids in Pearl's mane were all different sizes. Some of them were coming undone already, and the tangle of different-colored ribbons in Pearl's tail looked as if they

had been tied on at the very last minute. "What's happened here?" said Ms. Rosemary, holding up Pearl's tail.

A few of the students giggled. Rosa cringed. She couldn't imagine anything worse than a teacher pointing out her mistakes in front of the whole class. Poor Matilda! But Matilda didn't look upset.

"Sorry, Ms. Rosemary," said Matilda, pulling a small sketch pad out from her pocket. "But I was just about to do Pearl's tail when I saw a robin land on the ribbon box. He was trying to pull out some ribbon, and he looked so cute I just had to draw him. Look." She held out the picture. She had perfectly captured the little robin's silly expression.

Ms. Rosemary seemed to soften slightly. "It's an excellent drawing, Matilda, but you are here at the academy to learn how to care for your unicorn, not to draw robins. You must try harder,

or you won't graduate at the end of the year. Do you understand?"

"Yes, Ms. Rosemary." Matilda pushed her tangle of red hair off her face and sighed. "It's just that sometimes my fingers feel like they have to draw, but I'll try to stop them."

Ms. Rosemary smiled and moved on.

"Shall we do something fun together when the grooming inspection's over?" Rosa whispered to Crystal.

"Ooh yes! How about we go to the playground?" Crystal said, her ears pricking.

"Or we could go on the Safari Trail," said Rosa. "It goes all around the academy grounds. Apparently there are fox cubs, cave spiders, and if we're very lucky, we might even see a purple badger."

"Okay, let's do that," said Crystal. "We can visit the playground another time."

"We could ask the rest of the dorm to come with us too," said Rosa. She'd been really excited about making friends at the academy, but so far the others in her dorm had been quiet. The boys in Topaz dorm were often seen galloping around the grounds together, and the girls in Ruby dorm were usually in a big giggling group, but the students in Diamond dorm weren't like that. They were all quite different and most of the time went off on their own.

*Well, not anymore,* Rosa decided. *It's time we all had some fun together!*

Rosa waited for Ms. Rosemary to finish her inspection and dismiss the class. Then she stood on an upside-down bucket and clapped her hands together.

"Listen up, Diamond dorm! Crystal and I think we should all go on the Safari Trail together."

The four other girls from Diamond dorm

stared at Rosa. She squared her shoulders and smiled boldly back at her roommates, even though her heart was beating in double time. *Have confidence!* That's what Rosa's mom was always telling her. "It'll be fun!" she declared.

"We'll come, won't we, Twinkle?" said Violet, pushing her dark braid over her shoulder.

"Definitely," whinnied Twinkle, her unicorn.

Whisper nudged Ariana eagerly.

"Whisper and I will come too," Ariana said.

"And me and Pearl," said Matilda. She took off her glasses to polish them, and a pencil that had

been behind her ear fell to the ground. "So that's where I put it!" she said, pouncing on it. "Look! I thought I'd lost it!" She beamed as she stood up with her pencil.

The other girls giggled, except for Ariana, who just rolled her eyes. She was very organized and didn't have much patience with scatterbrained Matilda.

Rosa felt very relieved that the others seemed to like her idea. She'd felt nervous about standing up in front of them all. "Freya?" she called, her confidence increasing. "What about you and Honey? You'll come too, won't you?"

Freya was staring at one of the carts that moved around the stables, filled with sky berries for the unicorns to eat.

"Earth to Freya. Are you even listening to me?"

Freya jumped as Violet nudged her. "What's that?" she asked, looking around.

"Diamond dorm are going to ride the Safari Trail. Do you want to come with us?" Rosa repeated.

"No, thanks." Freya took out a tiny notebook from her pocket and began scribbling inside it.

"But you have to!" Rosa demanded, excited by her success with the other girls. "We're all going. You have to come."

"Let's go with them—please, Freya!" begged Honey, Freya's unicorn.

"Sorry," said Freya, barely glancing up. "I'm too busy."

Honey looked very disappointed.

"We'll come with you. Jester and I love outings. Where are we going?" Miki, a small boy with a playful smile, peered at Rosa through his long black bangs as he stopped on his way past them. His unicorn, with its shaggy dark blue mane and exceptionally long tail, nodded enthusiastically.

"Thanks, Miki, but maybe another time? This outing is for Diamond dorm only. We're *all* going," said Rosa, looking pointedly at Freya. She jumped off the bucket. "Come along, everyone!" She led the way outside, but as everyone regrouped in the courtyard, Rosa noticed that Freya and Honey had stayed behind in the stables.

"Freya!" she shouted in exasperation.

"She's not coming," said Miki, cheerfully tagging along with the group. "How about Jester and I pretend to be Honey and Freya?" He mimed opening a notebook and frantically writing something inside it.

Everyone laughed, even Rosa, who couldn't help but feel frustrated with Freya. How would the girls in Diamond dorm ever become best friends like the girls in Ruby dorm if Freya refused to do things with the rest of them?

"Sorry, Miki, but this is a Diamond dorm outing, and you're in Topaz. It has to be Freya and Honey. You and Jester can come next time," she said.

"Okay, then," Miki said. "Come on, Jester. Let's go and explore the gardens." He gave a dramatic sigh. "All on our own!"

Rosa felt bad, but she really wanted this to be a bonding experience for Diamond dorm.

"Freya . . . ," Rosa began, looking pleadingly to the blond girl who had now come outside.

"Nope," Freya said as she walked past, her hair flowing down her back. "I told you—I'm busy. Stop being so bossy."

Rosa felt her face redden, but she quickly recovered when Violet sent her a friendly smile.

"Freya really is busy," Violet confided. "She told me the stable carts had given her an idea for something she wants to build. Something that moves! You know how much she loves anything to do with engineering."

Rosa frowned. She didn't care if Freya built a hundred moving things. How could going off on your own be as much fun as spending time with your roommates and their unicorns? "We'll just have to go without her then," she said, rather angrily. "The Safari Trail starts in the orchard near the river. That's where the red bills are supposed to be nesting. Get in line, everyone. Stay behind Crystal and me, and don't forget to be quiet!"

Rosa and Crystal led the way through the apple trees to the stream at the bottom of the orchard.

It was one of many brightly colored streams that crisscrossed Unicorn Island, carrying the magical waters that nourished the land. The multicolored water came from the center of the earth, right there on the grounds of Unicorn Academy. It flowed up through a glittery fountain and into Sparkle Lake, before starting on its journey around the island. Rosa almost had to pinch herself. It was hard to believe she was really here, at Unicorn Academy, and training to be a guardian of Unicorn Island.

"I hope we do see a red bill," Rosa said to Crystal.

"We should if we're quiet," Crystal reassured her.

Rosa loved wildlife and had always wanted to train to be an island guardian. It had been a dream come true when she received the letter inviting her to Unicorn Academy.

Most students were at the academy for a year

before they graduated. Some got to stay longer if their unicorns needed more time to discover their magic power, or if they hadn't bonded with their unicorn. Rosa ran her fingers through Crystal's shimmery silken mane. Bonding was the highest form of friendship possible, and Rosa would know that it had happened because a lock of her own straight black hair would turn the same shimmery purple as Crystal's mane. Rosa couldn't wait for that to happen!

"Red bills, two of them, and a chick, over there," hissed a voice, startling Rosa out of her thoughts.

In the middle of the stream, two red bills were fussing around a chick as it swam out of the reeds and splashed in the water. Rosa held her breath. The fluffy chick with its enormous red beak kept sneaking away from its parents to explore. Then the parents would chase after it, squawking with alarm, and herd it back. The second the parents saw the girls approaching, they fled, hustling their chick into a reed bed and vanishing out of sight.

Rosa smiled at the sight, and then turned to see who had spoken to her. "Miki!" she exclaimed, seeing the dark-haired boy. "What are you doing here? This is a Diamond dorm ride," she added accusingly.

"I told Miki he could come with us after all," Violet said quickly.

Rosa frowned. She was in charge of this expedition, not Violet.

"Sorry, Rosa," Violet rushed on. "But please let him stay. He knows a ton of stuff about the countryside. His parents keep a herd of reindeer in the northern part of the island. Miki spends a lot of time watching the wildlife while he's minding the herd. Don't you, Miki?"

Miki's brown eyes twinkled mischievously as

he nodded. "You'd have missed the red bills if I hadn't pointed them out, Rosa."

Miki's smile was so infectious that Rosa couldn't help smiling back. "Okay, you can stay," she agreed. "But no taking over. This ride was my idea, so I'm in charge!" She beamed happily. She loved being the leader! "Come on, everyone. We're going to have some fun!"

## CHAPTER 2

The Safari Trail was a huge success. Miki, Violet, Ariana, and Matilda chatted all the way back, saying what a wonderful time they'd had. Rosa felt happy as they rode back to the stables. The only thing that bugged her was that Freya hadn't come too. How would Diamond dorm ever get to know each other and become friends if Freya kept refusing to join in? It wasn't fair to Honey, Freya's unicorn, either. She'd clearly wanted to come along.

Rosa felt very sorry for Honey as they arrived back at the stables. Honey was standing sadly in her stall, all on her own. She whinnied to them as they clattered inside.

"Did you have a good time? What did you see? I want to know all about it! Oh, I wish Freya and I had come too!"

While Rosa brushed the dirt from Crystal's silky coat, Crystal told Honey all about the trail ride. Honey hung on Crystal's every word.

"You should get Freya to join in more," Rosa told her.

"I try," said Honey sadly. "But she won't listen."

After Rosa had settled Crystal with a large bucket of sky berries, she went inside. As she entered the academy buildings she noticed that the door to the Great Hall was open. The hall was one of Rosa's favorite rooms, and she couldn't resist peeking inside. A ray of sunlight lit a path on the floor, drawing her in farther. The hall had a domed roof that was made of colored glass, and the rays of light shining through it made rainbow-colored swirls on the floor. Rosa's eyes fell on the center of the room, where the magical map stood. It was an exact replica of Unicorn Island in miniature, with tiny green valleys, golden beaches, and secret forests. Rosa went closer.

"You've heard the news, then?"

"Freya!" Rosa hadn't heard the other girl coming up behind her. "What news?"

"Didn't you even notice the force field wasn't working?" Freya said. "Didn't you wonder why you could walk all the way up to the map?"

Rosa realized that the humming, glimmering force field that normally protected the map wasn't there anymore. "I didn't," she admitted, mad at herself. She didn't like when she wasn't the first to discover something. "So, what's the news?"

"The force field isn't working because the magical map is broken. I just heard Ms. Nettles telling Ms. Willow, the new school nurse, about it. Ms. Nettles thinks that Ms. Primrose may have something to do with it. You've heard of Ms. Primrose, right? The head teacher who was here last year."

"Everyone's heard of Ms. Primrose!" said Rosa. Ms. Primrose and an unknown friend had tried to take control of the island by harming Sparkle Lake and Unicorn Academy. "It can't be her, though. She was caught and she's been locked up. My dad says that she's so well guarded that she'll never be able to harm Unicorn Academy or the island ever again."

"Yes, but my mom told me that before Ms. Primrose was captured, she stole the model of Unicorn Academy from the map." Freya pointed to a gap next to Sparkle Lake, where a tiny replica of Unicorn Academy should have been. "And, just now, Ms. Nettles told Ms. Willow she thinks that's why the map is broken. The map can take you anywhere on the island, but you need the model of the school to get back. The map is clever. It wouldn't take you on an adventure unless it was certain that it could get you back safely. Watch this." Freya leaned in. Touching a stretch of beach on the West Coast, she said, "I want to go to the beach."

"Freya!" Rosa gasped in alarm. What if the map suddenly whisked Freya away? The teachers would be furious. No one was allowed to use the magical map without Ms. Nettles's permission, not unless it was an emergency!

"See?" said Freya, her hand still touching the sand. "The map really is broken. I wish I could fix it."

"If all the staff can't fix it, what makes you think you could?" said Rosa.

Freya shrugged. "I'm good at fixing things."

"But it's a magical map," Rosa pointed out. "It will need magic to fix it." She heard a ringing. "There goes the dinner bell. We'd better hurry."

Freya was still staring at the map. Rosa tugged on her sleeve. "Come on, Freya. It makes all of Diamond dorm look bad if one person's late."

Freya shook her off. "When have I ever been late? You really are bossy, you know."

Rosa stared after Freya as she stalked off. She didn't know what it was about her and Freya, but the two of them always seemed to end up irritating each other.

In the dining room, Diamond dorm sat at the table next to the tall windows that overlooked Sparkle Lake. Everyone was talking about the magical map.

"I can't believe it's stopped working," said Ariana, helping herself to hot garlic bread, oozing with butter, from a basket on the table. "What if we need to get somewhere on the island quickly?"

Worry niggled in Rosa's tummy as she chased a strand of spaghetti around her plate. The map was important to the island's guardians, who needed to be able to react quickly if there was a problem on the island that required their help. What if something serious happened, and no one could get there in time to fix it?

"If the reason for the map not working is that Ms. Primrose stole the model of the school, then Ms. Nettles should make her give it back," said Rosa.

"Maybe Ms. Primrose doesn't have it anymore. Maybe she lost it," said Matilda.

"Like you would," Ariana muttered, with a swish of her braids.

Matilda grinned, not at all upset. "Yep!"

"Maybe she hid it," Violet suggested.

Rosa's eyes widened. "She might have. It might even be somewhere in the academy. We could try to find it. Think how thrilled Ms. Nettles would be if Diamond dorm got the map working again. All the teachers would be so pleased with us. Who wants to help me look?"

"I'm in," said Violet eagerly.

"Me too," said Ariana, and Matilda nodded.

"We could start by searching Ms. Primrose's

old study," said Rosa, her mind whirling. "There might be a clue there. Eat up, everyone, and no asking for seconds. We've got important work to do."

The girls ate quickly, except for Freya, who kept stopping to write in her notebook.

"Are you almost done?" Rosa asked her as everyone else stood up to leave.

"No," said Freya, not even looking up as she somehow managed to eat ice cream with one hand while sketching out a complicated-looking diagram with the other. "But you go on. I'm not coming."

"What a surprise!" said Rosa, annoyed. But Freya didn't seem bothered by her tone. She just kept sketching.

"Come on," Rosa said, turning to the others. "We'll see if *we* can find the model, because *we* care about the academy."

She stomped away from the table. Violet hurried alongside her. "Freya cares too," she said. "She just doesn't always like joining in."

"Hmm," said Rosa, raising her eyebrows in disbelief.

She led the others up the stairs toward the teachers' rooms. Rosa didn't know exactly where Ms. Primrose's old study was, but surely it couldn't be that hard to find, could it?

"Do you know where we're going?" Ariana asked as Rosa led them along the twisty corridors. "I'm sure we've passed that clock engraved with unicorns twice already."

"That was a different clock," Rosa lied. To her relief she suddenly caught sight of a door that had a faded nameplate on it saying MS. PRIMROSE. "Look, we're here. I told you I knew the way!"

Rosa pressed her ear to the dark wooden door and listened. The room sounded empty, just as she would have expected, but she knocked anyway, just to be sure. Then she opened the door cautiously. The study appeared not to have been touched since Ms. Primrose left. The walls were lined with bookcases and pictures of unicorns.

There was a large desk with pens spread over it, and a pile of books and papers. Behind the desk, there was a picture of a rearing unicorn, its head surrounded by a glowing mane and its haunches covered in a starry pattern. The chair was shoved back as if Ms. Primrose had just been called away for a minute. It made Rosa feel uneasy, but she pushed the feeling away. She was in charge—she had to seem confident!

"Everyone spread out," she whispered. "Remember, we're looking for a tiny model of the school."

"Look everywhere," Ariana added, her brown eyes serious. "It might be hidden in a secret drawer."

"That's exactly what I was going to say!" Rosa set to work at once, emptying the drawers of the large desk. She was disappointed not to find anything other than stationery and pens in any of the drawers. Rosa tapped the bottom of each one in the hope of finding a hidden compartment.

"Matilda!" hissed Ariana, who was taking books from a shelf and stacking them on the floor in neat piles as she worked her way along. "Don't dump those papers over here. You're messing up my system."

"Sorry!" Matilda pushed her red hair out of her eyes, leaving a smear of dust on her cheek. "Isn't this fun? Ooh, look at those glittery pencils. I'd love a set like that." She brushed past the pile of books as she hurried toward a set of silver and gold pencils lying on one of the shelves.

"Stop!" squeaked Ariana as a tower of books toppled over with a crash, taking a second tower down with it. "Oh, Matilda!"

"It's not as bad as it looks." Violet quickly dropped to her knees and began helping Ariana pick up the scattered books and papers.

Rosa came over to help. As she picked up a book, something small and silver fell out of it and landed on the floor with a clink. "What's that?"

"A key," said Violet, seizing it. "It's so tiny. I wonder what it's for."

Rosa took the key. It was slender, with a rearing unicorn key chain. The part that went into the lock was pointed and looked like a star. The rearing unicorn seemed familiar.

Rosa tapped the key in the palm of her hand as she tried to remember where she'd seen it before.

"That's it!" Her eyes fell on the picture hanging behind Ms. Primrose's desk. It was of a unicorn with a mane that looked like a halo. Excitement shivered in her tummy. "The picture and the key, they're the same!"

Rosa crossed the room. She wasn't sure what she was looking for, but she was certain the key and the picture were linked.

"Look at the stars!" she exclaimed.

The unicorn in the picture had a cluster of stars on its haunches identical in shape to the end of the key. Rosa squinted at them, and then she noticed that one had a small hole. She held the key up to the star, and it slipped inside. "It's a lock," she gasped.

The others crowded around as the key turned with a soft click and the painting swung slowly away from the wall, revealing a golden safe.

## CHAPTER 3

"Look at that!" Rosa stared at the hidden safe. She could hardly breathe she was so excited. Maybe they were about to find the model of the school!

"I bet it's locked," said Violet.

Rosa turned the dial. To her surprise, the lock opened immediately.

"Be careful," warned Ariana as Rosa opened the door and reached inside.

To Rosa's disappointment, there was no little model of the school inside the safe, just a large rolled-up piece of paper tied with a gold ribbon. "There's a scroll," she said, pulling it out. Curious, she undid the bow and went to the desk. She spread the paper out, anchoring the ends of the map with two picture frames to stop them from curling back up.

Everyone crowded around.

"It's a map of somewhere called the Glittering Cavern!" said Violet, pointing to a label.

"It's hand-drawn and very good," said Matilda appreciatively.

The map, neatly drawn in sparkling rainbow inks, showed an incredible ice cavern full of multicolored icicles and surrounded by a complicated maze of frozen passages.

"Look at those stalactites and stalagmites," breathed Rosa. "Did you ever see anything so beautiful?"

"Or dangerous," added Ariana, with a shiver. "Imagine if one of those stalactites snapped. It could spear you if you were standing underneath it!"

"See that?" Rosa made an excited stab at a tiny picture of a building marked with an X, right in the center of the cavern. "It's Unicorn Academy."

"What does it mean?" wondered Violet. "Why

would there be a drawing of the academy inside an ice cave?"

"Perhaps Ms. Primrose was planning on destroying the academy by freezing it in ice," said Matilda, her green eyes huge behind her glasses.

Rosa frowned. "Why would she do that?"

Matilda had pulled a pencil from one of her pockets. She chewed the end thoughtfully. "Um . . . Well, everyone said Ms. Primrose wanted more power. She did lots of terrible things before she was caught. Maybe that's why?"

But another idea was growing inside Rosa. "No, do you know what I think? This is more like a treasure map, and it marks the spot where Ms. Primrose hid the model of the school! That's why the academy is so tiny. It's not the actual school— it's the model!"

"Ooh yes!" said Violet. "I bet you're right."

Excitement fizzed through Rosa. "Imagine if we

followed this map and found it? Once the model is returned, the magical map will work again, and everyone will be so pleased with us!" She could hardly get the words out in her excitement. "Let's go to this Glittering Cavern and bring the model home!"

Ariana frowned. "It would be far more sensible to just give the map to Ms. Rosemary or Ms. Nettles. They'll know what to do with it and be able to go there and get the model."

"But think how much more fun we could have solving the mystery ourselves," said Rosa. "We could ask our unicorns to come with us. It would be a real adventure."

Matilda nodded. "It really would."

But Ariana shook her head. "It could be really dangerous."

"We don't need to decide right now," Violet said quickly. "Let's go back to the dorm." She glanced around and shivered uneasily. "I keep feeling like someone is watching us!"

"Okay," said Rosa. "We can continue talking in our lounge, where no one can hear us."

Rosa replaced the key in the book. Then, hiding the map under her thick school sweater, she led the girls out. Luckily they didn't meet anyone until they were near their dorm. As they rounded a corner, they saw Freya hurrying down the hall ahead of them.

"Freya!" Rosa called. "Wait up! We're going to our lounge. We've got something *really* important to discuss. Come with us!"

But Freya just disappeared around the corner. Disappointed, Rosa led the other girls to the Diamond dorm lounge. A fire was burning in the fireplace.

"I've got a bag of marshmallows somewhere," said Matilda. "Let's toast them."

While Matilda searched in her locker for the sweets, Rosa watched the flames leaping in the fireplace. The more she thought about her idea, the more sense it made. Ms. Primrose must have hidden the model in the Glittering Cavern. Why else would she have marked the map with a picture of the school and an X, and then hidden the map in a safe? They had to find it!

Matilda appeared waving a fat bag of pink and white marshmallows and a bundle of toasting forks. "Here we go!"

"Matilda, watch out!" said Ariana, ducking as Matilda almost poked her with the forks. "Here, let me give them out. No, not that one—that's your pencil!"

The girls giggled as Ariana removed a pencil from the middle of the toasting forks and gave it back to Matilda. She handed out the forks. "Remember, don't get too close to the fire when you toast the marshmallows," she warned everyone.

"Okay, so about the map," Rosa started as Violet passed around the marshmallows. "I've been thinking—"

"I'm not going," Ariana interrupted firmly, kneeling down by the fire. "I really think we have to tell the teachers."

"But that's boring!" Rosa protested.

"Look, it's too late to do anything now," Violet said. "Why don't we sleep on it and decide in the morning?"

Matilda and Ariana were already leaning forward and holding their marshmallows over the flames.

"All right," sighed Rosa. Squeezing between Matilda and Ariana, she banged her toasting fork down on the edge of the fireplace. "Okay, everyone. I've decided we won't do anything with the map until tomorrow. Until then, it's going to be a Diamond dorm secret. You are not to tell *anyone*," she added, giving them all an extra hard stare. "Is that understood?"

"Ooh, I do love a secret," said Matilda. "My big brother told me an amazing secret just before I left home to come here. If you promise not to tell—"

"Matilda!" Rosa interrupted. "A secret is only a secret if you don't tell anyone!"

Matilda turned pink. "I know," she said, with a guilty smile. "But none of you know my brother, so it won't matter if—"

"It does matter," said Rosa firmly, her gaze switching from Matilda to Ariana, who she thought was definitely the most likely to tell a teacher. "This map is Diamond dorm's secret. If anyone talks about it, especially to a teacher, then you'll have me to deal with!"

Matilda gave a squeak. "Scary!"

Rosa's fingers trembled as she pushed a marshmallow onto the end of her toasting fork. She was pleased how fierce she'd sounded, even though she'd felt anything but fierce inside. Violet was right. It was too late to do anything with the map now. But tomorrow was Saturday, and that meant they didn't have any lessons to go to. As soon as she had persuaded the others to do what she wanted, they could think up a way of getting to the Glittering Cavern. But first Rosa had another problem to solve. *Where* exactly on Unicorn Island was the Glittering Cavern? She didn't have a clue!

## CHAPTER 4

Rosa was up early the next morning, waking everyone up. "Today we're going to look for the Glittering Cavern!"

"Go away. I'm a bear. I'm hibernating," groaned Matilda, burrowing deep inside her blue-and-silver blanket.

But Rosa wouldn't leave Matilda alone. She tickled her until she finally sat up, reaching for her glasses, while Rosa flung the curtains wide, flooding the room with winter sunlight.

Rosa had loved Diamond dorm from the moment she'd first set eyes on it. It was a tower room. The five beds were arranged around the curved walls, and the girls slept with their feet pointing into the middle of the room. On the first day, Rosa had claimed the best bed nearest one of the windows, hurriedly emptying the contents of her overnight bag and putting her things in her wardrobe before any of the other girls arrived.

Each bed was covered with a blue-and-silver blanket. It had a small wardrobe on one side and a dresser on the other, with a lamp lit with a diamond so that each girl had her own light to read by. Rosa had made her area feel more homey by putting pictures on her dresser— one of her mom and dad, and another of her granny and grandpa. On her bed was a colorful silk elephant that Granny had made to remind her of

home. The other girls had pictures too, of parents, grandparents, siblings, and pets. Rosa wished she had a brother or sister, or even a pet.

Freya was dressed before anyone else. Tucking a notebook into her pocket, she hurried down to the stables. Rosa wanted to chase after her and get her to agree to come with them, but she was worried that if she did, Matilda would go back to bed, and then they would all be in trouble.

"I can't find my hoodie," said Matilda, hunting around.

"You should try hanging things up instead of throwing them on the floor," said Ariana, dumping a pile of Matilda's clothes that had crept into her space back onto Matilda's bed.

"Oh, thank you, Ariana. That's where my hoodie went," said Matilda, pulling it over her head and almost losing her glasses. "Whoops!" she giggled.

Ariana sighed.

At last everyone was ready, but as they walked to the stables, Rosa fell behind the others and slipped inside the hall to look at the magical map once more. It seemed so sad without the buzz of the magical force field. The hole where the academy should have been was like a missing tooth. Rosa reached out hesitantly and touched the map.

"Show me where the Glittering Cavern is," she breathed. "Please," she added hopefully. A tremble ran through her fingers. Rosa snatched her hand away. Was the map trying to work? What if it managed to take her to the Glittering Cavern? Without the model of the school to bring her back, she might be stuck there for good. Rosa pushed her straight dark hair behind her ears and bent to study the map again. The gap where the academy should have been was glowing.

*I think the map's asking for my help,* Rosa thought

suddenly. *I think it wants me to find the model of Unicorn Academy.*

"I will help you," she whispered. "Just show me where the Glittering Cavern is."

Another area of the map suddenly began to glow. It was a ridge of snowy mountains to the north of the academy. Rosa caught her breath. Was that where the Glittering Cavern was? The mountains looked like the kind of place where an icy cavern might be found.

The glow faded away, and Rosa was filled with a warm sense of duty and pride. The map had chosen *her* to help! *Well, I'm not going to let it down,* she thought.

She ran full speed to the stables, hoping to catch up to the others before she got there. But the rest of Diamond dorm were already there, and Rosa heard their cheers and shouts of laughter as she opened the stable door. A stream of bubbles drifted out, floating past her into the sky. There was another loud cheer. What was going on?

Rosa burst inside. The rich smell of burnt sugar hung in the air. Rosa immediately recognized the smell. *Magic!* Her mother's unicorn, Ace, was a fire unicorn, and whenever he did magic, the air smelled just the same. She saw a crowd of people gathered around Jester's stall.

"Jester's found his magic," said Violet, moving over to let Rosa in. "He's got bubble magic. It's the coolest thing ever. And Miki and Jester have just bonded—look at Miki's hair."

Rosa couldn't take her eyes off Miki. He was standing in the center of an enormous silvery bubble that wobbled and shimmered around him, so at first she didn't notice his hair. But there it was, a streak of dark blue that was just noticeable against his own black locks.

"Do it again," Matilda was begging. "Please,

Miki, do the bubble walk again. I want to sketch you."

"All right," said Miki. He placed his hands against the walls of the bubble. Then, pushing gently against it, he took a careful step forward. The bubble quivered. Rosa held her breath— was it going to burst? Miki pushed against the shimmering wall and the bubble suddenly tipped forward, rolling like a giant ball. Miki kept going, walking slowly, an enormous grin plastered on his face. As his confidence increased, he walked faster, rolling along until the bubble hit a broom propped against the wall. With a loud pop, it burst on the bristles, sending thousands of tiny bubbles drifting up into the air. Miki leaped onto Jester's back, and they took a bow.

Everyone clapped and cheered. "I can't wait to tell Mom and Dad," said Miki breathlessly. He couldn't stop smiling. "Bubble magic is awesome.

When Jester has practiced his magic more, he'll be able to make really strong bubbles. We can use them to protect the reindeer from wolves when we move them from their winter pastures to the summer ones."

Rosa clapped along with the other students even though she felt a bit jealous. Why hadn't she and Crystal bonded? They'd been friends from the moment they set eyes on each other. Rosa was also desperate to know what magic Crystal would have.

"Hurry up, Diamond dorm," she said. "We need to talk!"

"Can't we stay here a bit longer?" said Violet. "Jester's going to try to build a bubble bridge next."

"Great," whispered Rosa, rolling her eyes at Violet. "Let me know when he's finished. Then he can make a bubble road that leads to the

Glittering Cavern, because that's where we need to go instead of hanging around here in the stables! Come on, everyone," she ordered sharply. "There isn't time for this. We seriously haven't got a second to waste!"

## CHAPTER 5

"So, what do you think?" Rosa looked at her roommates. They were standing in a group outside the stables with their unicorns. She had even managed to make Freya curious enough to join them with Honey. "I'm sure the magic map gave me a definite sign that we should go to the Glittering Cavern. It's in some mountains that are not too far away. We could ride there in about four hours, I think. We could be back by dinner if we leave soon."

"I think we should go," said Violet. Twinkle nodded.

"I still think it's too dangerous," protested Ariana. "And it's a really long way."

"Please let's go," said Whisper, her unicorn. "It sounds really exciting."

"We'll vote," decided Rosa. "All those in favor of going to the Glittering Cavern today, raise your hands or nod your heads."

All the unicorns nodded enthusiastically and all the girls, except for Ariana and Freya, raised their hands. Freya hesitated for a moment, then nodded and raised her hand too. Honey whinnied in delight.

"It's decided then!" Rosa exclaimed. "We've voted and agreed. We're all going to try to find the Glittering Cavern—and the missing model of the academy."

"All right," said Ariana reluctantly. "But we must be careful, and what will we do about food?"

"I'll deal with that," Rosa declared. "Meet me

back here in an hour, and we'll set off then!" She was thrilled. Finally, Diamond dorm were going to do something all together, and just imagine how pleased the teachers would be if they came home with the missing model!

"You're the best, Rosa," Crystal said, nuzzling her as the others went off to get breakfast. "I love the way you organize everyone."

Rosa hugged her. "We'll find the model," she told her. "I know we will!"

Rosa arranged for the cook to give everyone a packed lunch and gathered together some blankets, packing them into a backpack with some rope and a compass.

At last they all set off, riding their unicorns northward, keeping on course with the help of Rosa's compass. All the unicorns seemed very excited to be riding out on an adventure. Rosa kept noticing a flurry of pink sparks swirling around Crystal's hooves as she trotted along. The February day was sunny and cold, but Rosa, in the lead, went at such a fast pace that it wasn't long before Crystal was thirsty.

"I need a drink," she declared, changing course and trotting toward a babbling brook at the far end of the meadow they were riding through.

"Water!" squealed Pearl, splashing straight into it with Matilda still on her back.

Rosa, Freya, Ariana, and Violet dismounted. Freya let Honey take a long drink while she stood with a faraway look on her face.

*I bet she's thinking about making some sort of machine,* thought Rosa, with a flicker of irritation. *Why can't she just focus on what we're doing now?*

Crystal finished drinking and shook her head, spraying everyone with rainbow-colored water droplets.

"Ahh!" screamed Matilda, getting splashed. "Water fight!"

"Yay! Water fight!" Pearl stamped her hooves in the brook.

Whisper created a mini whirlpool with his hooves as he kicked up the water.

"Stop!" cried Ariana desperately. "Please stop. Whisper, you're soaked. How can I ride you when you're that wet?"

Whisper was having too much fun to listen. He stamped a hoof, sending a wave of colored water cascading over Twinkle and Honey, and an even bigger wave over Crystal.

"Take that!" whinnied Crystal. Pink sparks swirled around her as she stamped in the brook, over and over again.

Rosa's nose wrinkled as she caught a whiff of something sweet in the air. "Crystal!" she gasped. "Look at you!"

For a second, Crystal was lost in a whirl of snowflakes that spun around her in a sparkling white mist. The unicorns stopped splashing and stared, their mouths hanging open in wonder. Gradually the snowflakes stopped spinning and melted away.

"That was awesome!" Pearl exclaimed. "Do it again."

Crystal seemed dazed. "W-w-what just happened?" she stuttered.

"You made it snow," said Honey, staring at Crystal's hooves. "I think you must have gotten your magic!"

"Did I?" Crystal lifted a hoof, holding it awkwardly as if it didn't belong to her. "I was just thinking how cold the water was and that it reminded me of snow."

"Do it again," urged Rosa.

Crystal concentrated hard and smacked her hoof into the brook. Snowflakes spun around like a mini whirlwind then danced along the surface of the water.

"Oh, Crystal," said Rosa, her breath catching. "You've definitely got your magic."

"Snow magic!" Crystal exclaimed, rearing up with her mane and tail streaming behind her. "Just the same as my grandma. I can't wait to tell her. This is my best day ever."

Matilda and Violet clapped and cheered as

Crystal cantered out of the water and Rosa threw her arms around her neck. Her unicorn had found her magic! The first of the unicorns in Diamond dorm! She felt like she was going to burst with pride. She sneaked a look at her hair. Had they bonded too, like Miki and Jester had? Her heart sank when she saw there was no colored streak in her hair. *Never mind.* Rosa shook off her disappointment. She was sure it would happen soon.

"You know what else I can do with snow magic?" Crystal said to Rosa.

"Er, build a snowman?" Rosa asked.

Crystal puffed out her chest. "No, silly, I can make a snow twister! It's a special kind of whirlwind made from magical snow that doesn't feel cold at all—in fact, it's lovely and warm. A snow twister can be used to move things from one place to another. I bet I can make a snow twister that will take us all to the Glittering Cavern!"

"Really?" Rosa gasped.

Crystal nodded. "Gather around. It's easier if we all stand close together."

"Are you sure this is safe?" asked Ariana.

"Perfectly! I've ridden in Grandma's snow twisters, and it's totally safe." Crystal fell silent as she concentrated on using her magic. Rosa laid a hand on her mane for encouragement as Crystal stomped on the grass with her hoof. "Take us to the Glittering Cavern!" she whinnied.

Pink sparks flared up then died away. Everyone looked at each other.

"Try again," urged Rosa. "You can do this, Crystal. You're the best unicorn in the world."

Tossing her mane in delight, Crystal banged on the ground again. This time, sparks crackled around her, twirling into the air, as a pink snow twister curled from under her feet and began to whirl in a tight circle around the girls and their unicorns. A dark curtain of silky hair blew over Rosa's face. Then her stomach swooshed as the snow twister swept her from her feet and twirled her high into the air. "We're off to the Glittering Cavern!" she cried.

## CHAPTER 6

Rosa clung to Crystal's mane, pink snowflakes spinning around her as the twister carried them all away. She was surprised how warm she felt. The snowflakes whirling around her face and catching in her hair were soft and cozy, like a fleecy blanket. All too soon, the twister slowed as it came back down. The snowflakes shimmered and turned clear. Then Rosa hit the ground with a jolt, tipping forward and landing on her knees.

"Whoops! Sorry about that," panted Crystal.

Rosa got to her feet and clutched Crystal's mane, her legs feeling wobbly.

"I think I might need to work on landings," gasped Crystal.

The others were picking themselves up beside Rosa. In front of them was a snowy mountain range. The ground they were standing on was frozen solid, covered with ice.

"We're really here," said Freya. "That was such cool magic, Crystal." She frowned. "Are you okay?"

Rosa looked at Crystal, whose sides were heaving. "You look exhausted," she said with concern.

"It was hard work," Crystal panted. "But I'll be fine in a bit."

While Crystal got her breath back, Rosa and the others gazed around.

"Look at that giant cave," said Violet, pointing. "Do you think that's the entrance to the cavern?"

Matilda went over and peered inside. "There

are lots of those long icicle things in here," she called. Pulling out her sketch pad, she started to draw.

The others joined her. The cave was enormous, with a high domed roof, silvery-white stalagmites twisting up from the floor, and pointed stalactites hanging from the icy ceiling, which glowed a silvery blue. Three tunnels led out of the cave. Rosa shivered into her hoodie as she pulled out the scroll taken from Ms. Primrose's study. "This must be *this* entrance here," she said, spreading the map on a nearby boulder and stabbing her finger at one edge of the drawing. "To get to the middle, we need to take the third tunnel."

Rosa started to roll up the map, but Freya stopped her.

"Wait, the picture doesn't match these tunnels. On the map, the passages twist away, but these tunnels"—Freya pointed ahead of her—"don't seem to twist at all. They each go in a straight line. I think we're at this entrance here," she continued, placing a finger on the opposite side of the map. "Which means we should probably follow the second tunnel."

"No, no, no. You're wrong," Rosa insisted. "The tunnels might start off straight, but I bet they then begin to twist."

Freya went over to the tunnels to investigate.

Crystal nudged Rosa with her nose. "Rosa, maybe you should listen to Freya," she said softly.

Rosa was surprised. Crystal never told her what she should do. "But I'm sure I'm right," she whispered.

"Rosa, these tunnels really do go straight into the mountain for quite a long way before they start to twist," said Freya, looking back over her shoulder. "That's not what the map shows."

Rosa realized everyone was looking at her. She

couldn't back down. "It's a hand-drawn map. It's not going to be that accurate," she said. "I'm good at map reading, so just trust me."

"Last week Ariana got the best grade on the map quiz Ms. Rivers gave us in Geography and Culture," Freya said. "Perhaps she should look at the map and see what she—"

"No!" interrupted Rosa forcefully. "I'm in charge of this adventure, and I say we go down this tunnel."

Crystal nudged her arm as if she wanted to say something, but Rosa ignored her. "This way, everyone!"

She vaulted onto Crystal and set off. Matilda and Violet shrugged and followed on their unicorns.

Rosa glanced back. Ariana and Freya were deep in conversation at the tunnel's entrance. "Hurry up or you'll get left behind," she shouted.

Ariana and Freya exchanged a look before
joining her with their unicorns. But the argument
had left an awkward feeling in the air, and now
they all rode in silence.

After a while, Rosa's teeth began to chatter. "If
only the passage was as cozy and warm as your
snow twister," she whispered to Crystal. "I wish
we could go faster."

"The path is too icy," said Crystal as she

carefully picked her way around the weirdly shaped stalagmites. "If we go faster, we'll slip and fall." She pulled up suddenly as the path split, one way rising up and the other sloping down. "Which way now?"

"That's easy," said Rosa. "The cavern is in the middle of the map and underground, so we have to go west, which is left."

"How do you know which side of the cavern we are on?" called Freya. "We might be on the other side, in which case we need to go east."

"I just know," said Rosa, frustrated.

"But you might be wrong," Freya pointed out.

"Fine, I'll show you the compass," sighed Rosa, wishing Freya didn't always have to argue with her. She pulled out her compass. "Oh, that's weird. The needle won't stay still."

"That is odd," said Violet. "The compass should work underground."

Ariana looked uneasy. "Magic can make compasses behave strangely. What if it's gone all crazy because of something magical? What if we're walking into a trap?"

Rosa laughed. "A trap? Why would Ms. Primrose leave a trap for herself? No, I think the compass must just have been damaged in the snow twister."

"But how could a snow twister damage it?" asked Freya.

Rosa didn't know, but she couldn't admit that. "I must have sat on it when we landed," she lied. "Come along. If we go down here, I'm sure we will reach the cavern soon."

"Rosa . . . ," Crystal began.

"It's okay, Crystal. I know I'm right," said Rosa, trying to sound confident.

But after continuing on for a very long time, riding through caverns and splashing through a stream, the tunnel they were in grew narrower and the ceiling lower so that the girls had to lean over their unicorns' necks to avoid bumping their heads. At the back, Ariana and Freya started whispering together again.

*Let them whisper,* thought Rosa. They'd soon be

thanking her when they reached the Glittering Cavern at the center of the ice maze. According to the map, they were almost there.

"Hurry," she whispered to Crystal. Rosa imagined how amazing it would be if they returned to school with the model. Suddenly a noise startled her out of her thoughts. It started like the rustle of wind through leaves, but it quickly grew to a roar. The tunnel turned even colder as the roaring noise came bowling toward Crystal and Rosa.

"W-what is it?" whinnied Crystal, stopping dead.

"I don't know. I—" Rosa broke off with a yell as a squeaking, whirring cloud of creatures came flying around the corner, filling the tunnel. Rosa felt icy cold as the black mass buzzed over and around her, wings snagging in her hair and tickling her ears. The air rang with high-pitched squeaks.

"What are they?" she yelled, batting the creatures away while shielding her head with her other hand.

"Ice bats!" Twinkle whinnied from behind them. "We must have disturbed their roost!"

Crystal and the other unicorns hopped from side to side to try to avoid the icy creatures.

"Everyone stay still," called Violet from the back. "The ice bats won't hurt us."

"They're sooo cold," gasped Ariana, her teeth chattering loudly.

As the stragglers passed over, the air grew warmer and the unicorns stopped jumping around. Rosa stroked Crystal's trembling neck. "It's okay," she soothed. "We can go on now."

"Those poor ice bats," said Crystal guiltily. "We

scared them away." She continued around the corner. "Look," she said as the tunnel ended in an icy wall covered with ledges jutting out. "This must be where they were roosting."

Rosa stared at the frosty wall ahead. They'd come to a dead end. She reached out and pushed on it with her hand as if it might suddenly melt away. "Is there definitely no way through?"

Crystal pushed the ice with her nose. "It's solid," she said. "We'll have to go back." Her eyes met Rosa's, and Rosa felt a sudden flicker of shame that she hadn't listened to Crystal.

"So, this isn't the tunnel we were looking for, Rosa?" called Freya.

"No," Rosa muttered, hating to admit that she'd been wrong. "We'd better turn around."

Slowly, the unicorns shuffled around. There wasn't much room, and Pearl got stuck when she tried to turn too fast. Then Matilda got stuck trying to dismount to help her and somehow ended up sitting backward on Pearl's back, facing her tail! Eventually Matilda managed to right herself, but then she got so muddled directing Pearl where to put her hooves as she turned in the tight space that Violet and Twinkle had to take over, calling out instructions for her. At last everyone was facing the right way, but now Rosa and Crystal were at the back of the group.

"Move over," said Rosa. "Let Crystal get to the front."

But no matter how the unicorns squeezed up, there simply wasn't room for Crystal to pass, and Freya had to take the lead. Disgruntled, Rosa rode at the back of the group until the path opened into a tiny grotto surrounded by frost-covered rocks. Rosa and Crystal joined the others as they stopped at the edge of a cluster of stalagmites.

"We're lost, aren't we?" Freya said.

Rosa dismounted and opened the map. It was beginning to crease, and the edge was torn. "No, we're not," she said, not wanting to admit she didn't have a clue where they were. "We're here." She pointed to a grotto marked on the map.

"I don't think we are, Rosa," said Ariana, looking at the map over her shoulder. "That grotto's bigger than this one and has only one path leading out of it. This one has two."

"First you led us to a dead end, and now you say we're in a grotto that's nothing like the one shown on the map," said Freya. "Admit it, Rosa— you don't know where we are."

Rosa's face flushed bright red.

"It's okay," said Ariana quickly. "I think we might still be able to find the Glittering Cavern.

The map shows a pool in the center of the cavern. It's fed by a stream. Water can't flow uphill. When we leave this grotto, we need to find our way back to the stream we passed earlier and follow the direction it's flowing in. It should lead us to the cavern."

"Luckily I made a list of identifiable things so we can retrace our steps," said Freya. She held up her notebook. "The path we need to get out of here has a stalagmite that's so tall it almost reaches the ceiling."

"I remember seeing that," said Rosa grudgingly.

Freya held out her hand. "Maybe if Ariana and I have the map, we might be able to find the cavern."

Rosa held on to the map tightly. She didn't want to hand it over. The adventure had been her idea. She wanted to be the one who found the model of Unicorn Academy and gave it to Ms.

Nettles. But there was no getting out of it—she'd gotten everyone lost. If she didn't let Freya and Ariana have the map and lead the way, they could be stuck here forever. Rosa shivered. She was sure it was getting colder.

Crystal nudged her. "It's the right thing to do, Rosa," she said, her dark eyes encouraging.

"Fine," Rosa sighed, handing the map over. "You two figure out the way."

## CHAPTER 7

With Ariana's excellent map-reading skills, Freya's useful notes, and the rest of Diamond dorm chipping in with helpful suggestions, it wasn't too long before the girls and their unicorns arrived at the center of the maze. As they stepped into the Glittering Cavern, everyone fell silent. They all stared in wonder at the enormous cave. Ice-white stalagmites spiraled upward to a ceiling embedded with tiny sparkling stalactites as bright and delicate as stars. Water tumbled down a pile of rocks into a glassy pool that shimmered with a blue hue, and icebergs floated across it, looking like giant water lilies.

Matilda's cheeks were turning pink. "Now what?" she asked, her teeth chattering noisily.

Rosa looked around the whole cave. She was convinced that the model was hidden here somewhere, but there were so many nooks and crannies she didn't know where to start her search!

"The model could be anywhere," she said. "Spread out and start looking."

The girls and their unicorns fanned out across the cavern.

"This could take ages," Crystal whispered to Rosa.

*And we might not even find it,* thought Rosa. The model could be hidden on any of the icy ledges, in one of the crevices, or even on top of one of the massive stalagmites. Rosa began to worry. How would they see the model if it was on top of a stalagmite, let alone reach it?

She and Crystal searched for ages, and Rosa had almost given up hope of ever finding it, when a flicker on the wall caught her eye. "Crystal, what's that over there? I can see something glimmering."

"It looks like a candle," said Crystal. Carefully, she stepped around an ice-covered rock to get a better look.

Suddenly Rosa noticed a hidden arch, dotted with tiny blue crystals, set in the cavern wall. "Look!" Her voice rose in excitement. "There's the model!" Relief flooded through her. They'd found the model! Hopefully now everyone would forget she'd gotten them lost. "Let's get it," she urged.

Crystal took a step closer, but as she did, something shifted under her hooves. She sprang back, almost unseating Rosa. Rosa hung on to Crystal's mane, her heart galloping. She knew she wouldn't hurt herself if she fell off—the island's magic would protect her, catching her in a giant bubble and floating her down to the ground. But island magic wouldn't save Crystal if she fell into the dark pool of water that had opened up inches in front of her hooves!

"Rosa! What happened?" asked Violet, riding over on Twinkle.

Rosa stared in surprise as the crack in front of them began to freeze over, concealing the water below. "I've found the model," she said. "It's up there. But it looks like it's been booby-trapped to stop anyone from taking it. If you get too close, the ice cracks."

Jumping from Crystal's back, Rosa selected a large stone from the frosty ground. "Watch this." She threw the stone onto the ground in front of the arch. A jagged line ran across the ice and it slid apart. With a plop, the stone fell into the dark water and disappeared.

Freya stared at the crack as the ice froze over again. "It looks like an enchantment. I have no idea how we can break it, though. We'll have to find a way to reach the model without touching the ice."

"Can that be done?" asked Rosa doubtfully.

"Anything's possible with engineering," said Freya. "If we had materials, we could build a bridge to reach it." She stared at the enchanted ice as if it might give her the solution.

Rosa was just about to suggest they return to the academy in one of Crystal's snow twisters and get some materials to build a bridge, when Freya suddenly spoke. "I've got an idea. It's dangerous, but it should work. It needs all of us to help, though. First I need your hoodies. I'm going to tie them together to make a rope that I'll fix around my waist like a lifeline. Then I'll run across the ice really fast, grab the model, and run back. If I'm quick enough, I think I can make it, but if I don't, then you must stop me from sinking by pulling on the rope of hoodies."

Ariana spluttered. "That's much too dangerous. Even if you don't drown, and you probably will, you'll get soaked. And then you'll freeze to death. Let's just go back to school and tell the teachers where the model is."

"But we're here now," said Rosa desperately. After coming this far, she couldn't bear the thought of pulling out and letting the teachers retrieve the model.

"Rosa's right," said Freya. "We can't go back without the model. Not when we're so close."

Rosa's eyes widened in surprise. She wasn't used to Freya agreeing with her!

"I don't mind getting wet," Freya went on, giving Rosa a quick smile. "And I'd like to know if my plan works. Please help us, Ariana."

Ariana shuddered. "I don't know why anyone would want to risk drowning in freezing-cold water, but if you insist on going through with this plan, then I suppose I'll have to help."

"Thanks, Ariana," said Freya. "Hoodies off, everyone, and give them to me."

"No, wait," said Rosa, suddenly remembering. She opened her backpack. "We don't need to use our hoodies. I brought a rope with me."

"You star!" exclaimed Freya. "That was brilliant thinking!" She lifted her hand and high-fived Rosa. "A rope will be much better."

"Maybe I should be the one who . . ." Rosa

was going to suggest that she go for the model instead of Freya, because she did really want to be the one who picked it up and brought it home, but she broke off as Crystal nudged her hand.

"Teamwork, remember!" Crystal whispered.

With a sigh, Rosa fell silent. Crystal was right. She loved taking the lead, but maybe some of the others did too and, as they'd already proved, her ideas weren't always the right ones. Rosa suddenly wondered if that was why Ms. Rosemary had stopped calling on her in class. Maybe she was letting the rest of the class have a turn.

She began to tie the rope around Freya's waist, but then Ariana took over because she knew a lot about different types of knots and how secure they were. Once Ariana was happy with how the rope was tied, she handed the end to Honey, who held it firmly between her teeth. Rosa organized everyone else in a line behind the unicorn.

"Ready?" Freya asked, taking up the slack of the rope.

"Ready!" they chorused back.

"Good luck!" shouted Rosa as Freya stepped onto the ice. With a deafening shriek the ice began to split, but Freya ran like the wind, sprinting toward the arch and snatching the model from the ledge. Black water bubbled up over the sides of the crack as it grew wider. Freya darted back, her hair flying out behind her and her eyes on the shore as she slipped and slid on the watery ice. The water was rising, sucking her down as it crept up to her ankles. Freya kept on going, arms flailing. She was almost at the shore when the ice gave way completely, tipping her into the murky water with a giant splash. Ariana and Violet both screamed, almost dropping the rope as Freya slipped under the water and out of sight!

## CHAPTER 8

Rosa leaped into action as the air filled with alarmed whinnies and yells.

"Pull!" shouted Rosa, her voice rising forcefully above the noise. "Everyone pull together. Get behind me and pull, right now! *Pull!*"

She leaned back, straining on the rope till her arms burned. The rope bit into her fingers, but she ignored the pain. The others heaved the rope too. The unicorns joined in, grabbing the rope with their teeth and pulling backward. As the rope tightened, Rosa, the girls, and the unicorns took one giant step back and then another. Rosa gritted her teeth, leaning back and pulling with all her might.

*Come on, Freya! Come on!* she willed.

Suddenly Freya's arm appeared through the ice.

"Again!" Rosa screamed. "Pull, everyone!"

A second later Freya's head popped up, then the rest of her came with it, flopping onto the ground with icy water pouring from her clothes.

Everyone gathered around while Freya coughed up the water she'd swallowed.

Rosa was full of wonder. "We did it," she exclaimed shakily. "We did it!"

Honey nuzzled up to Freya, breathing on her with her warm breath. The other unicorns did the same, but Freya was shivering badly.

"Wait, I think I can help by using a snow twister!" said Crystal. "It might warm Freya up." She took a deep breath.

"You can do it," Rosa told her, touching her neck.

Confidence flooded into Crystal's eyes. She stamped a hoof and a mini twister swirled around Freya, hiding her from view. The pink snowflakes worked their magic, warming Freya and drying her soaking clothes. As the snowflakes faded, Rosa saw that Freya's cheeks were pink again and she had stopped shivering.

"Thank you, Crystal!" Freya smiled.

Rosa hugged Crystal. "Are you okay?" she said, seeing that she was breathing heavily again.

Crystal nodded. "Making twisters is a lot of work, but it's fun!"

Rosa helped Freya to her feet. The girls' eyes met and they hugged.

"Thanks," Freya whispered in Rosa's ear. "I heard you shouting and telling everyone what to do. If you hadn't done that . . ." Her voice trailed off.

"I'm just glad you're all right," said Rosa, feeling a warm glow spread through her from her head to her toes. Maybe she and Freya could be friends after all—really good friends. Suddenly she remembered something. "The model!"

"What? This, you mean?" Freya grinned and opened her right hand. The model of the academy was nestling safely in her palm. The unicorns whinnied, and the girls whooped. "There was no way I was going to drop it," said Freya, inspecting it. "It's a beautiful piece of engineering. Look at how the doors and windows all open."

"Even better—it can get us back to school!" said Rosa.

"How does it work?" asked Matilda.

"I think we just tell it where we want to go," said Rosa. As she spoke the model started to glow.

Freya pushed the model into Rosa's hand. "Go on. You do it. You had the idea for this adventure. You should be the one to take us home." Everyone else nodded, and Rosa felt her heart swell with happiness as she looked around at Diamond dorm, all united for once.

Crystal nuzzled Rosa's cheek. "I'm so glad I'm paired with you."

Rosa hugged her. "That makes two of us. I wouldn't want any other unicorn but you. Now let's go home." She raised her voice. "Unicorn Academy!" she shouted. A fierce wind suddenly swirled around the cavern, whipping the girls' hair behind them. A second later they and their

unicorns were all swept into the air, and then Rosa's eyes blurred. With a chorus of squeals and whinnies, the girls and their unicorns were whisked away.

★

*BUMP!* Rosa landed on her bottom. *I'm sitting on grass,* she realized as the wind faded away. She saw they were on the lawn directly outside Ms. Nettles's study. As they all scrambled up, Ms. Nettles and Ms. Willow, the school nurse, ran out through the tall glass doors.

"Girls, what is the meaning of this behavior?" Ms. Nettles exclaimed.

"Ms. Nettles, I . . . ," Rosa began, then catching Crystal's eye, she grinned sheepishly. "Sorry, I mean *we*—all the girls in Diamond dorm— heard that the magic map was broken because the Unicorn Academy model was missing, so we thought we'd try to find it."

Rosa continued the story, inviting her roommates to chip in, while Ms. Nettles listened in silence. When they reached the end, Rosa handed the tiny model of the school to Ms. Nettles, and Freya gave her the map.

"Well," said Ms. Nettles, her glasses rattling on the end of her bony nose, "I really ought to be angry with you for breaking so many rules. Let me see"—she began to list them off on her fingers—"there was entering Ms. Primrose's study, which is out of bounds, taking the map, not to mention leaving school grounds without permission."

Ms. Willow tutted in concern. "Girls, you have been very bad, brave but bad. Both you and your unicorns could have been hurt. Ms. Nettles and I are going to have to keep a careful eye on you!" She tucked a stray blond curl behind her ear. "Ms. Nettles, they all look frozen. May I go and get them some mugs of hot chocolate?"

Ms. Nettles smiled. "I think that would be an excellent idea, Ms. Willow. Girls, don't think that I'm not grateful," she continued as Ms. Willow hurried away. "The magical map will most definitely work now that it's complete again. But Ms. Willow is right—I shall be watching you all *very* closely in the future." Her lips twitched as if she was trying not to smile. "No more dangerous adventures from now on, at least not without asking my permission first. Now off you go. Take your unicorns back to the stables. Rosa, nice teamwork today. And well done for bonding with Crystal."

"Thank you, Ms. Nettles. . . . Wait, have we

bonded?" As Rosa turned her head to look at Crystal, a shimmer of purple caught her eye. She grabbed at the lock of hair, the exact same color as Crystal's mane, and stared at it in wonder.

"Crystal, we *have* bonded!" Rosa threw her arms around Crystal.

Ms. Nettles finally stepped in and shooed everyone back to the stables.

Rosa and her friends settled the unicorns with a huge feast of sky berries.

"You look tired," said Rosa, stroking Crystal's neck.

"I am tired," said Crystal happily. "But this has been my best day at Unicorn Academy so far. My magic is awesome, but the best thing was bonding with you, Rosa. You're my best friend ever."

Crystal stamped her hoof, sending a whirl of pink sparkles into the air. A flurry of snow fell,

landing on Rosa and Crystal in a frosty white
heart shape.

"Aw," said Rosa, with a giggle. "You're my best
friend too." She dropped a kiss on Crystal's nose.
"We make a great team."

Rosa gave Crystal one last hug, then she
ran after her friends back to Diamond dorm,

where steaming mugs of hot chocolate topped with whipped cream, chocolate sprinkles, and marshmallows were waiting for them.

"I know, let's have a feast!" said Matilda. "I've got cookies somewhere." She dived into her wardrobe and began pulling out sweaters and odd socks.

"I've got cupcakes," said Rosa, heading for her wardrobe.

"I've got candy," said Violet.

"Toffee popcorn, anyone?" called Ariana, producing an extra-large bag.

"And I've got a box of chocolates," said Freya, shyly producing a long box.

"To the girls in Diamond dorm and our unicorns," said Rosa, holding up a mug of hot chocolate. "Here's to our next exciting adventure."

The girls clinked their mugs together. "To our next exciting adventure!"

The animals are running away from
the forest, and everyone is worried.
Can Ariana and Whisper help
the animals get back home?

Read on for a peek at the next book
in the Unicorn Academy series!

Ariana woke to the sound of her unicorn alarm clock whinnying good morning. She stretched out a hand and switched it off, then carefully folded back her blue-and-silver blanket and swung her legs out of bed. Her toes sank into something soft, and she frowned. What was that? Leaning over, Ariana saw Matilda's hoodie crumpled on the floor.

"Matilda!" Ariana sighed, looking across at the girl in the next bed. Even in sleep, Matilda somehow managed to make Diamond dorm look messy. Her red hair was spread over her pillow in a sea of tangles, and her blanket hung from the edge of the bed.

As Ariana picked up the hoodie, a large spider with red stripes on its back scuttled across the sleeve. Ariana squealed and flung the hoodie back down, waking Rosa, Freya, and Violet.

"Ariana, are you all right?" said Violet, sitting up quickly.

"What's going on?" demanded Freya.

"Why did you scream?" said Rosa.

Only Matilda was still asleep, snoring softly.

"There's a sp-sp-spider," Ariana stuttered, pointing at the floor where the spider was picking its way over Matilda's hoodie. "I don't like spiders."

"Is that all?" Rosa groaned, flopping back against her pillow.

"Poor spider. It's probably trying to find its way outside," said Violet, pushing

★ ★ ★

her dark braid over her shoulder and going to investigate.

"Let's help it," said Freya, joining her. Gently, she scooped the spider up in her hands. "Aren't the red stripes on its back unusual? I've never seen one like it before. Open the window for me, Ariana."

Ariana stared at Freya in horror. What was she doing picking it up? Red meant danger, didn't it? What if the spider bit her?

"The window, Ariana!" Freya said impatiently.

Ariana hurried to the window and flung it wide open. She shrank back as Freya passed her, just in case the spider tried to escape. "Be careful!"

Freya rolled her eyes. "I can't believe you're scared of spiders. It's not going to hurt us. Surely you know there are no dangerous spiders on Unicorn Island?"

Ariana bit her lip, not wanting to admit she

didn't know much about creepy-crawlies. She just knew she didn't like them!

Freya held the spider as it sent out a thread of silk and sailed down the wall, but before she could close the window, Ariana saw a small emerald-green lizard climbing up the side of Matilda's wardrobe.

"Watch out!" she shrieked.

"Ariana, don't freak out. It's just a harmless lizard," said Violet. She caught it and put it on the windowsill. "It's very pretty. I wonder where it came from—and the spider."

"Probably from Matilda. She's so messy!" said Ariana, feeling better now that the spider and the lizard were safely outside the dorm. "I bet she brought them in on her clothes. They're always covered in grass and stuff. Look—" She gestured toward the dirty clothes around Matilda's bed. "No wonder our dorm is full of bugs."

"Bugs? Who's got bugs?" Matilda yawned and opened her eyes. Reaching for her glasses, she accidentally knocked over her lucky duck toy. It immediately started quacking. "Whoops!" She picked it up and turned it this way and that. "I can never remember how to make this stop," she said, frowning.

Rosa buried her head under her pillow with a groan. "Turn it down!"

"Good thinking!" said Matilda cheerfully. She shoved the duck under her pillow, muffling the quacking noise. "So, what's going on?" she said, putting her glasses on and looking around at them all. "Why's the window open? It's freezing."

"A spider and a lizard decided to spend the night with us. We were just putting them outside," said Freya, shutting it.

"It's probably your fault." Ariana frowned at Matilda. "I bet they came in on your clothes and you didn't even notice. You're so messy! You really should fold your things and put them away." Matilda flopped back with a sigh, sending the toy duck shooting out from under her pillow. Its loud quacks sent Rosa, Freya, and Violet into a fit of giggles. Ariana felt hurt. She'd hoped the others would back her up. Surely they couldn't enjoy sharing a dorm with someone as messy as Matilda?

As Ariana turned away, Violet put a hand on her arm. "Don't be upset, Ariana. I expect Matilda forgot to clean up last night because she was working on a picture."

"I was, actually," said Matilda, her long red hair falling over her shoulders as she nodded earnestly. "My little cousin was so excited when I told her all about being at school here. I promised I'd draw her a picture of our dorm. I've got it here somewhere, if you want to see." Matilda almost knocked a glass of water over as she began to sift through a pile of paper balanced on her dresser.

"You can show me later," said Ariana shortly. She sat down at the mirror. Her black hair was braided with colorful beads. She checked the beads were secure and tucked some braids behind her ear. Whatever Violet said, it wasn't just last night that Matilda had forgotten to put her clothes away—she always forgot, and it was really annoying! Back at home, Ariana lived with just her mom and dad, and they were very clean and organized—just like Ariana. She had packed and repacked her suitcase several times before she left home to come to Unicorn Academy. She had been really looking forward to it, but she was finding it hard living in a dorm with four other girls, particularly messy Matilda.

Remembering the angry look Freya had given her when she'd carried the spider to the window, Ariana felt her stomach twist. Making friends was turning out to be so much harder than she had imagined. She hadn't thought the other girls would be so different from her! Violet was easy to get along with, but Freya spent much of her time alone with her engineering inventions, Rosa always wanted to have adventures, and Matilda was annoyingly messy and scatterbrained. *I wish they were more like me,* thought Ariana wistfully. *I don't really feel like I've got any friends here at all.*

# READ MORE ABOUT

UNICORN ACADEMY

# New friends. New adventures.
# Find a new series . . . just for you!

**ISADORA MOON**
For ballerina and fairy and vampire lovers

**MAGIC ON THE MAP**
For adventurers

**UNICORN ACADEMY**
For unicorn lovers

**PUPPY PIRATES**
For dog lovers

**PURRMAIDS**
For mermaid and cat lovers

**BALLPARK Mysteries**
For sports fans

RHCB rhcbooks.com

# PUPPY ☠ PIRATES

**Ahoy, mateys!**
**The treasure hunt for your next**
**favorite book ends here!**

## PUPPY ☠ PIRATES

### Stowaway!

Wally is a pup with a nose for adventure!

Erin Soderberg

rhcbooks.com RHCB